D1708465

h!

team

These quotations were gathered lovingly but unscientifically over several years and/or contributed by many friends or acquaintances. Some arrived, and survived in our files, on scraps of paper and may therefore be imperfectly worded or attributed. To the authors, contributors and original sources, our thanks, and where appropriate, our apologies.—The Editors

CREDITS

Compiled by Dan Zadra

Designed by Steve Potter

ISBN: 978-1-932319-73-6

 Contact: Compendium, Inc., 600 North 36th Street, Suite 400, Seattle, WA 98103. Team, Good Life, Compendium, Celebrating the joy of living fully, live inspired and the format, design, layout and coloring used in this book are trademarks and/or trade dress of Compendium, Incorporated. This book may be ordered directly from the publisher, but please try your local bookstore first. Call us at 800-91-IDEAS or come see our full line of inspiring products at www.live-inspired.com.

1st Printing. 15K 09 08

We are
the ones
we've been
waiting for.

JUNE JORDAN

THERE IS SOMEBODY SMARTER THAN ANY OF US, AND THAT IS ALL OF US.

MICHAEL NOLAN

NO ONE CAN BE

THE BEST AT EVERYTHING.

BUT WHEN ALL OF US

COMBINE OUR TALENTS,

WE CAN AND WILL BE THE BEST

AT VIRTUALLY ANYTHING.

DAN ZADRA

A star team will always
beat a team of stars.

BEN WALLACE

FOCUSED

ACTION

BEATS

BRILLIANCE

ANY DAY.

ART TUROCK

Surround yourself with optimistic, forward-looking people.

ZIG ZIGLAR

When building
a team,
I always search
for people
who love to win.
If I can't find
any of those,
I look for
people who
hate to lose.

ROSS PEROT

I am looking for

a lot of people

who have an

infinite capacity

to not know what

can't be done.

HENRY FORD

THE REAL WINNERS
IN LIFE
ARE THE PEOPLE WHO
LOOK AT EVERY
SITUATION WITH AN EXPECTATION
THAT THEY CAN
MAKE IT WORK OR MAKE
IT BETTER.

BARBARA PLETCHER

Winners say,
"It may be difficult,
but it's possible."
Losers say,
"It may be possible,
but it's too difficult."

BOB MOAWAD

Losers say,
"Let's see
what happens."
Winners say,
"Let's make
it happen."

BOB MOAWAD

Champions are
their own experts.
They want
to know,
"Who says so?"
When someone
gives them
five good reasons
why they can't,
they look for
ten good reasons
why they can.

ROB GILBERT

HELP EACH OTHER BE RIGHT, NOT WRONG. LOOK FOR WAYS TO MAKE NEW IDEAS WORK, NOT FOR REASONS THEY WON'T. DO EVERYTHING WITH ENTHUSIASM— IT'S CONTAGIOUS.

ANTHONY PIVEC

Excellent organizations and teams are experimenters supreme.

TOM PETERS

THEY TRASHED THE RULES AND FOUND NEW WAYS TO WIN.

MARK ROMAN

Ignore people who say it can't be done.

ELAINE RIDEOUT

Working together, ordinary people can perform extraordinary feats. They can push things that come into their hands a little higher up, a little farther on towards the heights of excellence.

B.J. MARSHALL

Anything
one person
can imagine
other
people
can make
real.

JULES VERNE

Great teams cultivate
HOW thinkers, not IF thinkers.

FRANK VIZZARE

Champions
do not
believe
in chance.

ROB GILBERT

LUCK IS THE RESIDUE OF DESIGN.

BRANCH RICKEY

RESIGN AS GENERAL MANAGER OF
THE UNIVERSE AND TRUST YOUR TEAM.

LARRY EISENBERG

If people are coming to work excited... if they're making mistakes freely and fearlessly...if they're having fun... then somewhere you have leaders.

ROBERT TOWNSEND

Don’t expect

team players

if you haven’t

made it a

team sport.

BARRY MAHER

JUST GETTING PEOPLE IN
THE SAME PLACE
AT THE SAME TIME DOES NOT
PRODUCE A TEAM.
COMMUNITY REQUIRES A
COMMON VISION AND
SHARED VALUES.

DIANE DREHER

Superior
work teams
recognize that
consistently high
performance
can be built
not on rules
but only on
values.

DENNIS KINLAW

IT ISN'T COMMON GROUND THAT BONDS
PEOPLE TOGETHER, IT'S HIGHER GROUND.

TOM BROWN

Great teams set aside personal agendas to focus all their resources on a common goal.

AL SCHMITT

Part of

team success

is understanding

that there's

something bigger

and more important

than ourselves.

MARCIA ANN GILLESPIE

STRATEGY IS NOT
SOMETHING THAT'S DONE IN
A BOX WITH ONLY A RATIONAL
HAT ON. IT NEEDS TO BE
VISCERAL, HUMAN, AND OFTEN
EMOTIONAL—AND EVERYONE
MUST BE INVOLVED
IN CREATING IT.

ROBERT STONE

MY IDEA OF A SUCCESSFUL MEETING IS WHEN SOMEBODY ATTENDS AND SAYS, "I COULDN'T TELL WHO WORKED FOR WHOM."

CHUCK BEYER

OUR SUCCESS
MULTIPLIES
EACH TIME
WE LEAD SOME-
ONE ELSE TO
SUCCESS.

SUSAN COLLINS

If we make our customers important, they will inevitably return the favor.

DON WARD

Your customers aren't customers anymore. Your vendors aren't vendors anymore. They're either your teammates or someone else's teammates. If you're not on their team, they'll find someone who is.

JOHN ELLIS

Empower every
member of your team.
Celebrate their
successes.
Eliminate bureaucracy.
Accommodate
your customers.
No exceptions,
no excuses.

JOHN KANE

If you're not serving the customer, you better be serving someone who is.

KARL ALBRECHT

If you want to attract the best and the brightest, then you have to build an organization you feel good about.

WILLIAM C. FORD, JR.

Integrity is not negotiable.

PAT "PK" KORAN

You don’t always have to like each other, but you have to trust each other. When my team calls on me, I’ll be ready. When they put the ball down, I’ll kick it through.

GEORGE BLANDA

Trust each other again and again. When the trust level gets high enough, people transcend apparent limits, discovering new and awesome abilities for which they were previously unaware.

DAVID ARMISTEAD

THERE ARE NO GOLD MEDALS FOR THE 95-YARD DASH.

MAX DEPREE

We are judged by what we finish, not by what we start.

SUSAN FIELDER

The first rule of survival is clear: Nothing is more dangerous than yesterday's success.

DAN ZADRA

WE ARE FOREVER IN A STATE OF CHANGE, FOREVER BECOMING.

SIMONE DE BEAUVOIR

School is never out for the professionals.

JIM WILLIAMSON

Every day, in every

way, I'm getting

better and better.

ÉMILE COUÉ

There are many compliments that may come to an individual in the course of a lifetime, but there is no higher tribute than to be loved and appreciated by those who know us best.

DR. DALE E. TURNER

To keep that good feeling
you get from a sincere compliment,
pay one to someone else.

DON WARD

Greatness is a perception. It may or may not be reality yet. What is important is that the quest for this reality is shared by many other people.

CHARLOTTE CHANDLER

Don't work for
my happiness,
my brothers—
show me yours—
show me that
it's possible—
show me your
achievement—
and the
knowledge will
give me courage
for mine.

AYN RAND

The best companies assume that each individual wants to make a difference in the world and be respected. Is that a surprise?

PAUL AMES

A COMPANY SHOULD STAND FOR SOMETHING, FULFILL A PURPOSE, AND CONTRIBUTE SOMETHING USEFUL—HOPE-FULLY SOMETHING SPECIAL, EVEN WONDERFUL—OR IT SHOULDN'T BOTHER BEING A COMPANY AT ALL.

DAN ZADRA

Every man is entitled

to be valued by

his best moments.

RALPH WALDO EMERSON

MAKE THE
WORLD
BETTER.

LUCY STONE

Never doubt
that a small group
of thoughtful,
committed people
can change
the world. Indeed
it is the only thing
that every has.

MARGARET MEAD

"How can I help you?" is a question we ask our customers every day; I believe it's a question we should be asking our teammates every day, as well.

RON KENDRICK

What have you done for your team today?

WILLIAM PLATT